Librarian Reviewer
Chris Kreie
Media Specialist, Eden Prairie Schools, MN
MS in Information Media, St. Cloud State University, MN

Reading Consultant
Elizabeth Stedem
Educator/Consultant, Colorado Springs, CO
MA in Elementary Education, University of Denver, CO

First published in the United States in 2007
by Stone Arch Books,
151 Good Counsel Drive, P.O. Box 669,
Mankato, Minnesota 56002.
www.stonearchbooks.com

First published by Evans Brothers Ltd,
2A Portman Mansions, Chiltern Street,
London W1U 6NR, United Kingdom.

Library of Congress Cataloging-in-Publication Data
Lawrie, Robin.
    Cheat Challenge / by Robin and Chris Lawrie; illustrated by Robin
Lawrie.
        p. cm. — (Ridge Riders)
    Summary: Slam and the father of his arch-rival, Punk, have both seen
the course of a new cross-country bicycle race before it is announced, and
Slam must decide whether or not to tell his friends and start practicing
there, even though logging in the area would make it dangerous to do so.
        ISBN-13: 978-1-59889-347-2 (library binding)
        ISBN-10: 1-59889-347-5 (library binding)
        ISBN-13: 978-1-59889-442-4 (paperback)
        ISBN-10: 1-59889-442-0 (paperback)
        [1. All terrain cycling—Fiction. 2. Bicycle racing—Fiction.
3. Cheating—Fiction. 4. Logging—Fiction.] I. Lawrie, Chris. II. Title.
PZ7.L438218Che 2007
[Fic]—dc22   2006026632

1 2 3 4 5 6 12 11 10 09 08 07

Printed in the United States of America

The Ridge Riders

 Hi, my name is "Slam" Duncan.

This is Aziz. We call him Dozy.

Then there's Larry.

This is Fiona.

And Andy.

* I'm Andy. (Andy is deaf. He uses sign language instead of talking.)

CHEAT CHALLENGE

by Robin and Chris Lawrie
illustrated by Robin Lawrie

STONE ARCH BOOKS
MINNEAPOLIS   SAN DIEGO

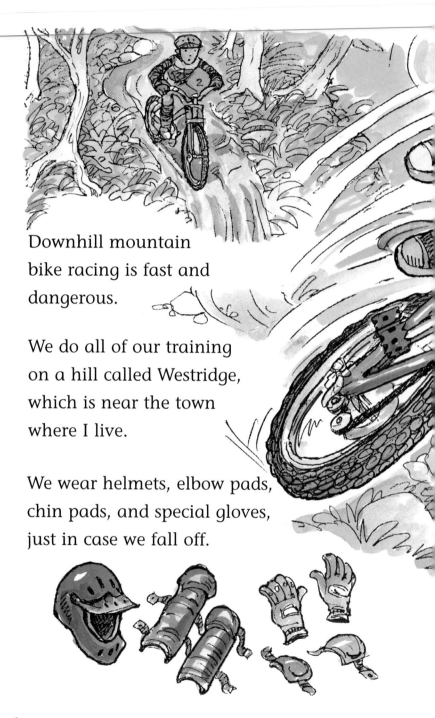

Downhill mountain bike racing is fast and dangerous.

We do all of our training on a hill called Westridge, which is near the town where I live.

We wear helmets, elbow pads, chin pads, and special gloves, just in case we fall off.

It happens!

Oooh!

We race
against the clock.
The fastest time down
a course is the winner.
The courses are about a mile long.

Although Westridge looks like a forest, it's really a big tree farm. Some of the trees are harvested every ten years or so, and new ones are planted in their place.

Big machines are used to cut and stack the trees. If you are smart, you stay far away!

So we did.

Cross-country bike racing (Xc) also takes place on Westridge. Cross-country racers don't race against the clock. They race against each other!

They wear tight shorts and t-shirts, even in the winter. Their bikes are very light and the riders are in great shape.

They have to be because the courses can be six miles long and they sometimes go around two or three times!

One day, Larry and I were training on the cross-country side of Westridge, far away from the tree cutters. We overheard some cross-country racers talking.

Yeah! Excalibur's really hard!

Yeah, I've heard it's pretty tough!

So how come it's just for kids, then?

13

When they weren't having battles, Arthur and his knights would have jousts, which were like pretend battles. The idea was to knock the other guy off his horse, and if he was not hurt, you could have a sword fight.

They also had helmets and body armor, but made of steel, not plastic.

15

On the way home,
Larry went too far into
a corner.

He went crashing through the undergrowth and hit something very solid.

BANG

We pulled away the bushes to see what it was. And were amazed to find . . .

Excalibur!

A wooden one!

This must have been what those cross-country guys were talking about.

But what does it mean?

Larry, of course, had
to try pulling it out.

Nothing. Not an inch.
Then me.

No future kings here!

When we got to Larry's house, he
had some mail.

NATIONAL CYCLING FEDERATION PRESENTS

Sword in the Stump
CHALLENGE
MOUNTAIN BIKE RACES

To promote fair play and
understanding between cyclists

✓ 2 CROSS-COUNTRY RACES
✓ 2 DOWNHILL RACES
✓ 2 DUEL DESCENDERS

FEATURING!
eXcalibur
the new Xc course.
It's eXciting

Later that week, I was helping out in my dad's garage.

* Bob Turner — ace pro mountain biker and race course designer.

While I was vacuuming,
guess what I saw on the back seat?

eXcalibur (top secret)

FINISH

What luck! Now that I knew where the course ran, the team could get in lots of practice! But then I started thinking.

It wouldn't be fair. It would be cheating!

Suddenly, I sensed somebody behind me.

Well well, what's all this? Looks like the new Excalibur course. This'll have to be our little secret.

It was my arch rival "Punk" Tuer's dad! He had just stopped to get gas.

Punk Tuer is a good biker but also a terrible cheater. His dad would certainly tell him where the new course was.

Hey, Punk, guess what?

Sure enough, next weekend Punk and his friend "Dyno" Sawyer were practicing the right course.

Fiona, Larry, Dozy, and Andy thought that the new course followed the old 1990 course, because "90" is XC in Roman numerals.

What should I do? Should I tell them?

The problem was, the old "90" went straight through the tree-cutting area.

I was so confused.

Then it happened.

BANG

Larry rode straight into a log lifter.

Oh no, oh no, oh no! The poor boy is dead!

I was sure he was dead. The driver was sure he was dead.

25

So when Larry suddenly sat up,
the driver passed out.

THUD

That wasn't all. We were trying
to wake up the driver.

Then the tractor
started to roll
toward some hikers!

Oh no . . . !

Suddenly, Andy burst through the clearing and jumped into the cab.

ANDY!

I could see him quickly pulling all the levers, looking for the brake.

Mutter mutter yak yak.

I was signing and yelling at him, **"It's on the floor!"** but he didn't see and couldn't hear. The hikers were busy chatting and didn't hear me either.

Then things got really messy.

They just didn't understand.

The hikers apologized and were nice to Andy.
I was still upset, so I just rode away.

I rode till I found the sword in the stump at the end of the new course.

Okay, Excalibur, what would Arthur do now? I've tried not to cheat and four people almost got killed. Punk Tuer is cheating and is practicing on the new course. It's not fair.

Then I heard someone laughing. Bob Turner and his friends were marking the course with tape. The big secret was out. I didn't need to worry anymore.

They'll need super-glued saddles to stay on here!

HAW HAW!

Soon, everybody was practicing the new course.

LOYALTY · HONOUR

Wait a minute. Punk and Dyno were doing this course yesterday. How did they know?

Punk's dad saw the map, and so did I.

WHAT?

You did? I almost got killed! Why didn't you tell us?

If I blabbed and one of you won next week, we'd all be cheaters! Don't you see, fairness is what Excalibur is about! If we win, it'll be because **WE'RE THE BEST!**

WHICH WE ARE!

FAIR PLAY

About the Author and Illustrator

Robin and Chris Lawrie wrote the *Ridge Riders* books together, and Robin illustrated them. Their inspiration for these books is their son. They wanted to write books that he would find interesting. Many of the *Ridge Riders* books are based on adventures he and his friends had while biking.

Robin and Chris live in England, and will soon be moving to a big, old house that is also home to sixty bats.

Glossary

arch rival (ARCH RYE-vuhl)—one's main opponent or enemy

deaf (DEF)—not being able to hear well or to hear at all

Excalibur (eks-KAL-ih-bur)—King Arthur's sword

harvested (HAR-vist-id)—cut or gathered up

lever (LEV-ur)—a bar or handle that controls a machine

new-fangled (noo-FAYN-guld)—something that is new and different from what one is used to

Roman numerals (ROH-muhn NOO-mur-uhlz)—letters used by ancient Romans to represent numbers. For example, on some clocks V is 5 and X is 10.

undergrowth (UHN-dur-grohth)—areas of thick plants, especially under trees

yakking (YAK-ing)—talking a lot

Internet Sites

Do you want to know more about subjects related to this book? Or are you interested in learning about other topics? Then check out FactHound, a fun, easy way to find Internet sites.

Our investigative staff has already sniffed out great sites for you!

Here's how to use FactHound:

1. Visit *www.facthound.com*

2. Select your grade level.

3. To learn more about subjects related to this book, type in the book's ISBN number: **1598893475**.

4. Click the **Fetch It** button.

FactHound will fetch the best Internet sites for you!

Discussion Questions

1. What would you have done if you found the map of the new course, like Slam did? Would you have told your friends? Do you think he did the right thing? Do you think Punk's dad did the right thing? Explain.

2. Do you know any other stories about King Arthur? Talk about them.

3. On page 32, Slam says that fairness is what Excalibur is about. He also says that if the Ridge Riders win without cheating, it will be because they are the best. Talk about this. What would it mean if Punk and his team won?

Writing Prompts

1. Slam and the other Ridge Riders love to hang out on Westridge. Do you and your friends have a special place like Westridge? Write a description of it, being sure to include colors, sounds, and things you see there. If you're feeling creative, draw a picture!

2. On pages 12-15, the story of King Arthur is pictured. What is one of your favorite classic stories? Try creating your own illustrated version of that story.

Read other adventures of the Ridge Riders

Snow Bored

The Ridge Riders are bored. So much snow has fallen on their mountain biking practice hill that they can't ride. Luckily, Dozy has a great idea. He turns an old skateboard and a pair of sneakers into a snowboard. Before long, everyone is snowboarding.

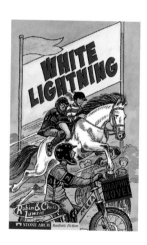

White Lightning

Someone smashed the Ridge Riders' practice jumps, and they suspect Fiona and her horse-riding friends. The boys are so mean to Fiona that she leaves. Then Slam gets a flat tire and has to race back home to get his spare, and he only has 50 minutes! Now a horse would come in handy!

Radar Riders

The Ridge Riders need a new place to race, so they build a wild new course. It takes all their skills, and some techno-wizardry, to keep them on track before they run into some unexpected turns.

Fear 3.1

While rock climbing, Slam loses his foothold. Luckily, his safety harness holds, but that doesn't stop Slam from being terrified. Soon, he can't even manage to complete the mountain biking courses he's ridden on for years. Will Slam ever get over his fear?

Check out Stone Arch Books adventure novels!

Blackbeard's Sword
The Pirate King of the Carolinas

Blackbeard holds the Carolinas in a grip of terror. Lieutenant Maynard and his men of the Royal Navy are after the pirate. They enlist the aid of young Jacob Webster and his father, but Maynard doesn't know that Jacob thinks Blackbeard is a hero!

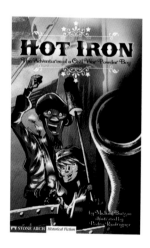

Hot Iron
The Adventures of a Civil War Powder Boy

Twelve-year-old Charlie O'Leary signs aboard the USS Varuna as it steams its way toward the mouth of the Mississippi River to fight the Confederate Navy. Will his ship survive the awesome Battle of New Orleans?